Penguin's *Adventure*
in Alphabet Town

by Laura Alden
illustrated by Jenny Williams

created by Wing Park Publishers

ℙ CHILDRENS PRESS ®
CHICAGO

Library of Congress Cataloging-in-Publication Data

Alden, Laura, 1955-
    Penguin's adventure in Alphabet Town / by Laura Alden ;
illustrated by Jenny Williams.
       p.   cm. — (Read around Alphabet Town)
    Summary: Penguin meets "p" words on her adventures in
Alphabet Town. Includes activities.
   ISBN 0-516-05416-3
   [1. Alphabet—Fiction. 2. Penguins—Fiction.] I. Williams,
Jenny 1939- ill. II. Title. III. Series.
PZ7.A3586Pe 1992
[E]—dc 20   92-1068
                                              CIP
                                              AC

Penguin's *Adventure*
in Alphabet Town

You are now entering Alphabet Town,
With houses from "A" to "Z."
I'm going on a "P" adventure today,
So come along with me.

This is the "P" house of Alphabet
Town. Penguin lives here.

Penguin likes everything that begins
with the letter "p."

She likes

pepperoni pizza.

And she likes to play the

piano.

Most of all, Penguin likes parades.

Once a year, Penguin plans a parade
for Alphabet Town.

Each year, she asks her friend

Pig

to help her. Penguin always says,
"Please." And Pig always says, "Yes."

This year, Penguin blows up

purple

and

pink

balloons for the parade.

Pig makes

popcorn

to sell, and tries not to eat it all.

Penguin also asks the painters of
Alphabet Town to help.

The painters paint signs and put
them all over town.

The parade begins! There are

puppies,

panda bears,

and even a parrot.

Police officers march in the parade too.

Here comes Penguin's Pots and Pans
Band! Pans crash! Pots smash!

18

BONG

CLASH

THUMP

CRASH

Penguin's band plays on and on and on.

A crowd watches the marchers and players.

They throw pennies into pails to pay for the parade.

They also buy

popcorn

and
peanuts

and pretzels too.

POP!

Some take pictures of the parade.
Penguin poses for a picture. Pop
goes the flash of the camera.

Now the parade is ending. The
mayor gives Penguin a present to
thank her for planning the parade.

It is a set of pretty marking pens.
"Thank you," Penguin says. Everyone
cheers.

Now it is time to go home. It is
time to pack up the pots and pans,

the peanuts and popcorn, and the
pails full of pennies.

Penguin puts her new pens in her

purse.

Then she starts for home.

Penguin's parade is over — at least until next year.

MORE FUN WITH PENGUIN

What's in a Name?

In my "p" adventure, you read
many "p" words. My name
begins with a "P." Many of my
friends' names begin with "P"
too. Here are a few.

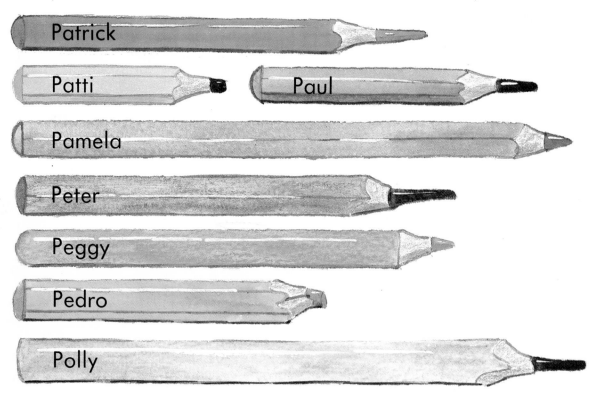

Patrick

Patti

Paul

Pamela

Peter

Peggy

Pedro

Polly

Do you know other names that start with "P"?
Does your name start with "P"?

Penguin's Word Hunt

I like to hunt for "p" words.
Can you help me find the words
on this page that begin with
"p"? How many are there?
Can you read them?

pie

cup

pancakes

balloon

zipper

mop

newspaper

pickle

Can you find any words with "p" in the middle?
Can you find any with "p" at the end?
Can you find a word with no "p"?

Penguin's Favorite Things

"P" is my favorite letter. I love
"p" things. Can you guess why?
You can find some of my favorite
"p" things in my house on page
7. How many "p" things can you
find there? Can you think of
more "p" things?

Now you make up a "p" adventure.